★ American Girl™

WellieWishers™

Willa's Butterfly Ballet

Adapted by Judy Katschke
from the screenplay by Dev Ross

Scholastic Inc.

It's a sunny day in the garden. The WellieWishers are exploring.

Camille notices how tall the sunflower has grown. She notices something else, too.

"Hey, over here," she calls to her friends. "Come look at these strange leaves!"

Kendall, Ashlyn, Emerson, and Willa run over.

"Those aren't leaves," Willa says. "Those are chrysalises. Caterpillars make chrysalises when it's time to turn into butterflies."

"Wait," Emerson says. "You mean there are caterpillars in those chrysalises right now, but when they come out, they will be butterflies? No way!"

"Yes!" Willa says. "And see those colors on the bottom? Those mean it's almost time for the butterflies to come out!"

Ashlyn gets excited. "Let's do
something special to celebrate
when the butterflies come out!"

"Like a dance," Camille says.

"Yes!" Willa says. "And we can call it the Butterfly Ballet!"

"And we can make butterfly costumes," Kendall says. "With wings that really flap!"

"Look!" Willa says. "There are five chrysalises. One for each of us!"

All five WellieWishers choose a butterfly to welcome.

Suddenly, one of the chrysalises wiggles.

"We better hurry and get ready!" Willa says. "It looks like the butterflies will come out soon!"

At the playhouse, the girls make butterfly wings.

"Bingo-bango," Kendall says. "Ready for liftoff!"

"It's time to practice our ballet," Ashlyn says. "But where's Willa?"

"I'm over here," Willa calls.
She's hanging from a tree!
"What are you doing?" Ashlyn asks.

"I'm practicing," Willa answers.
"My dance starts with an upside-down wiggle." She swings on the branch.
Uh-oh.

SPLAT!

Willa slips and lands in the mud.

Camille gasps. "Oh no! Your wings are torn and dirty."

"Squirrel sticks!" Willa says. "They're ruined!"

"Maybe we can help," Emerson says.

"I have a plan," Ashlyn says.

"Kendall will help Willa fix her wings.

"Camille and Emerson will watch for the butterflies to come out.

"And I will help everyone stick to the plan!"

Emerson and Camille go back
to the sunflower to watch for the
butterflies.

Soon, one of the chrysalises
wiggles!

"I'll go get the others,"
Emerson says. "Try to keep the
butterflies from coming out until
we come back!"

She runs off.

"How do I keep the butterflies from coming out?" Camille asks.

But Emerson is gone.

Camille thinks a lullaby might keep the butterflies asleep.

"Please stop wiggling, no more jiggling," she sings.

Back in the playhouse, Kendall helps Willa fix her wings.

"They aren't perfect," Willa says. "But maybe my butterfly won't mind."

All of a sudden, Emerson bursts into the playhouse.

"The butterflies are almost here!" she shouts.

But when the door opens, it bumps Kendall. She drops Willa's wings!

The paint smears into a big mess.
"Oh no!" Willa cries. "I can't meet
my butterfly wearing these. I'm not
going to the Butterfly Ballet."

"It won't be as fun if we don't
all dance together," Ashlyn says.
But Willa is too sad to dance.
"I'll just watch," she says.

The friends make it to the chrysalises just in time!

One butterfly comes out.

"Look!" Ashlyn says. "That's mine."

A second butterfly comes out.

"Amazing," says Camille.

A third butterfly comes out.
"Hello there, little buddy,"
Kendall says.
A fourth butterfly comes out.
"Beautiful," Emerson says.

Emerson, Kendall, Camille, and
Ashlyn twirl and flutter with the
new butterflies.

But Willa is still sad.

"My wings are a mess,"
Willa says. "And my chrysalis
is still closed."

"Look, here comes your
butterfly!" cries Kendall.

She points to the fifth
chrysalis.

The chrysalis wiggles.
"You can do it," Willa says.
"Come on out, little butterfly!"
Finally, a tiny creature flies out.

This butterfly looks different
from the others.

Its wings are not orange. They are
brown!

"Hey," Willa says. "This isn't a
butterfly! This is a cute little moth!"

"Look, Willa," Ashlyn says. "Its wings are brown, just like yours!"

"I guess my wings aren't so bad after all," Willa says. "In fact, they're perfect!"

"I'm going to show my moth my best boogie ever!" Willa says.
She begins to dance.
The WellieWishers laugh.
Soon, everyone is dancing for joy with their butterflies or moth!

Willa follows her moth around the garden. She skips, spins, and smiles.

Her friends are here.

She made a new moth friend, too.

That makes today a perfect day in the garden!

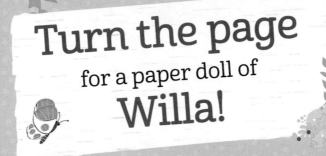

Turn the page

for a paper doll of
Willa!

Willa

Safety first!
When you see this symbol, be sure to ask an adult to work with you.

To dress your Willa paper doll:

1. Ask an adult to help you carefully cut out the clothing and accessories. Be sure to cut along all solid black lines, including slots.

2. Fold the tabs on the dotted lines and attach the clothing and accessories to your paper doll. Some tabs have slots to connect them together to help the clothes stay on better.

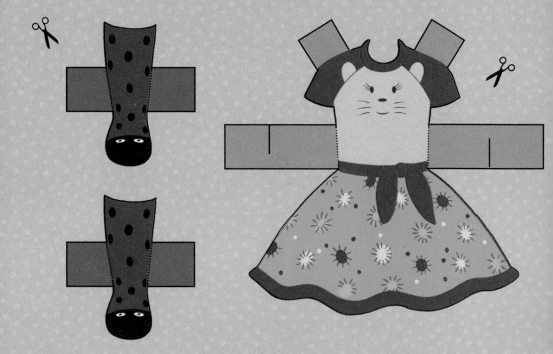

To attach Willa's wings:

1. Make sure Willa is wearing her outfit first.

2. Fold along the dotted line on the wings, then slide the slit at the bottom of the wings onto the outfit tab on Willa's back, like in the photo.

Want more clothes for Willa?

1. Use the cut-out clothes as stencils to trace blank clothes on paper.

2. Use colored pencils, markers, or even glitter and stickers to design your own outfits!

3. Ask an adult to help you cut out the clothes. Don't forget to leave tabs!

To put together your paper doll and stand:

1. Carefully press out the Willa figure.

2. Press out the two rectangular pieces. These will be the stand for the doll.

3. Find the slots labeled C on the stand pieces and fit them together.

4. Fit slots A and B on the stand pieces into slots A and B under Willa's feet.

5. Now you are ready to dress and accessorize Willa!

C

A

B

C

A ©/TM 2018 American Girl B